Library of Congress Cataloging-in-Publication Data

Gackenbach, Dick.
Timid Timothy's tongue twisters.

Summary: Several tongue twisters present the
stories of a fisher named Fischer, Betty Botter, a
tutor who tooted a flute, and others.
1. Tongue twisters.   [1. Tongue twisters]   I. Title.
PN6371.5.G33 1986   818'.5402   85-30531
ISBN 0-8234-0610-5

Timid Timothy's Tongue Twisters

ADAPTED AND ILLUSTRATED BY

Dick Gackenbach

HOLIDAY HOUSE / NEW YORK

See how Timothy's tongue is tangled and twisted?
Did these tongue twisters tangle and twist it?

Read on...

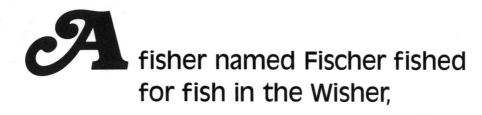
A fisher named Fischer fished
for fish in the Wisher,

but a fish with a grin
pulled young Fischer in.

Now fishermen fish the Wisher for Fischer
and wish that poor Fischer had
not fallen in.

Betty Botter bought some butter.

"But," she said, "the butter's bitter.

If I put it in my batter,
it will make my batter bitter.

But a bit of better butter,
that would make my batter better."

So she bought a bit of butter
better than her bitter butter.

And she put it in her batter
and the batter was not bitter.

So 'twas better Betty Botter
bought a bit of better butter.

A tutor who tooted a flute

tried to tutor two tutors to toot.

Said the two to the tutor,

"Is it harder to toot or
to tutor two tutors to toot?"

If Moses supposes his toeses are roses,

then Moses supposes erroneously,
for nobody's toeses are posies of roses,
as Moses supposes his toeses to be.

 maid with a duster made

a furious bluster dusting some busts in the hall.

When the busts they were dusted,

the busts they were busted,
the busts they were dust, that is all.

Now does your tongue tickle like Timid Timothy's?
Is it all tangled and twisted?
Then read this book backward
and untangle the twists,
it's the only sure way to untwist it!